Spooks

First published in Great Britain by
Granada Publishing in 1983
First published in Picture Lions in 1985
This edition published in 1992
10 9 8 7 6 5 4 3 2
Picture Lions is an imprint of the Children's Division,
part of HarperCollins Publishers Limited,
77-85 Fulham Palace Road, Hammersmith,
London W6 8JB

ISBN 0 00 662576-2

Produced by HarperCollins Hong Kong

Spooks

By Colin and Jacqui Hawkins
and a ghost writer

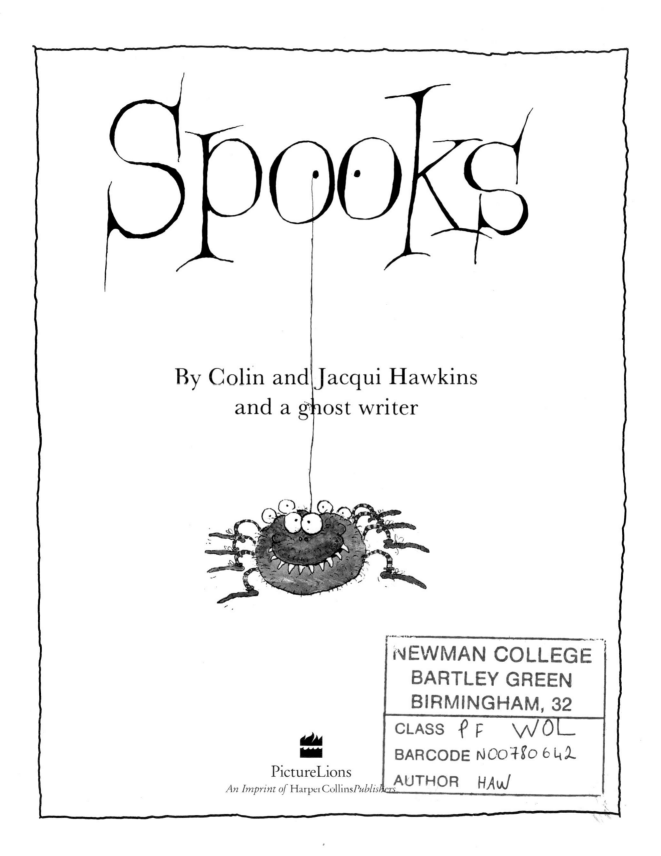

PictureLions
An Imprint of Harper Collins*Publishers*

Ghosts...

are just like
you and
me except
that....

..now you see
them......
and now
you don't .

Ghost Guises

Ghosts mostly appear as floppy white sheets. (They are said to materialize). Other spooks take different shapes. These are some you may – or may not – see.

Regular sheet ghosts (wraiths)

Several ghosts together are known as a shriek of ghosts.

Headless spook.

Bodiless spook

Terrifying ghost.

Terrified ghost

Spook Species.

Spooks can never change. When they return from the dead to haunt the living, they come as they were in life.

Accompanied by his faithful haggis, a Scottish spook plays his ghastly pipes as he stalks the castle battlements.

Irish Banshee

A miserable creature with bad news to tell.

Oh dear Oh dear 'tis a terrible ting... a terrible ting

Wail Wail Whine Whine

Screech! Screech!

Howl!

Can't see yoo, Jimmy

'Ay the Booo

The Tartan Torment

The Phantom of the Opera.

Heiaha!

Scandinavian Spooks.

all pulling together after centuries of pillage and plunder

At the Palace of Versailles, Marie Antoinette endlessly offers her crumbling cake to not so poor tourists.

Aimez vous le gâteau?

I 'ave met my Waterloo but.... 'as anyone seen Josephine?

Animal Apparitions

Even spiders may be spooks?

A har. Jim lac A har'

'Ghastly grim and ancient raven' — guarding ancient treasure

Cor! Stone the crows! I'm not that bad!

An Old Sea Dog

Sailors do tell of wild stormy nights when the only sound is that of the tap tapping of an old sea dog on the way to his drinking bowl in the seaport tavern.

A Famous Phantom.

The Flying Dutchman

Condemned to sail the seven seas forever, the Dutchman brings death and destruction to all who witness the passing of his ship, so DON'T LOOK AT THIS PAGE

Dick Turpin, on his famous mare Black Bess, preys on those with full piggy banks at lonely zebra crossings.

The loneliest Roman of them all searches for his legion 2000 years too late.

Another Famous Phantom.

Your piggy or your life.

A totally unknown phantom

Quo vadis?

'Or your sugar lumps'

Spook horse shoes get a lot of wear.

Spook Spotting

The lights dim, a freezing draught of air whistles under the unopened door, you hear footsteps coming towards you, nearer, nearer, nearer, the dog whines, the door handle turns and . . . you think you've seen a ghost? Don't kid yourself, it's not that easy. Spooks are no fools. You have to be really smart to spot a spook.

Most spooks are snobs, so don't bother spook spotting in high rise flats or council estates. Go to posh places where there are large old houses.

'Sit Sirrah.'

Woof!

Typical Elizabethan mansion spook with cur.

Remember: You'll never find a spook in a semi.

Heads are frequently carried because of the low ceilings.

Lots of monks, nuns and vicars become ghosts. So always look in churches and convents. Nuns and monks wear flapping garments for most of their lives so they are well equipped when they die. Listen for their chilling chant as they float about the cloisters a little above the cold stone floors, telling their beads.

As well as being snobbish, spooks tend to be set in their ways – they always remain at the level they knew. This only presents problems when the floor level rises rather than falls over the centuries and we witness the phenomenon of the footless ghost.

Ghostly Habits

Mother Superior. & (floats higher than the other sisters.)

A pair of holy ghosts

Father O'Flaherty fresh from the flames of hell.

Straying balls are a constant nuisance.

Transports to Terror

You are walking alone along a country road. It is dark and silent, except for the rustle of horse chestnut leaves and the thud of a falling conker. Suddenly you hear the thunder of hooves, the jangle of a harness, the creaking of coach wheels. Can this be the last bus?

Cold and tired you get out the fare, but DO NOT press your silver into the conductor's icy hand. Do not be tempted. For no-one returns from a lift in the headless coachman's carriage.

Hunting the Haunting

Are you brave? Could you sit in a dark cold crypt full of scuttling spiders, with slimy things slithering across the floor and gruesome ghouls moaning and groaning and dragging their chains and creeping up behind you. If so, spook spotting is for you.

Apart from nerves and guts all you need is a pig or cat and a few essential aids.

Pen with ink - Ghosts like writing messages

Candle in holder and lots of matches *

* Ghosts love blowing candles out.

Ball of string to find your way out of haunted houses.

Egors a Sissy.

Typical Ghost message.

Spook Spotter's Guide.

Apparitions to Zombies

Successful photo of spook.

Lots of humbugs - Spooks favourite sweets.

The O'Gools

Ghosts never move. They haunt the places in which they lived.
The O'Gools are typical. They try not to disrupt the nice
people who now live in their house but every so often one of
them slips up and gets seen. Screams, tears, terror – if only the
living knew how harmless these ghosts are:

For a start there's Dad, Mr Fingal Drool O'Gool, once a head
teacher but a shadow of his former self. Then there's Mummy,
Ginny O'Gool, whose fondness for spirits is famous, the older
children Ralph the Wraith and Mona the moaner, the identically
ghastly twins, Float and Gloat, and the pets Hairy and Scary.

Mummy and Daddy teach the young ones how to haunt
without hurting. But Ralph and Mona enjoy throwing on a
sheet and shocking half the neighbourhood. It's hard to keep
them home at nights. Even the pets like to pop up in
unexpected places and petrify the population.

"There's a poo in the loo
it must be you."

Float

Gloat

High Fibre Diet

At night, when the real family have gone to bed, the O'Gools materialize for breakfast. They need building up to keep fit for haunting. Like ghosts themselves, ghost food has no substance and does not comply with the law of gravity.

Nor, under the influence of the children, does the furniture. Ghosts learn to levitate when they are very young and making other objects rise into the air is the favourite game of spook children. Objects flying about a room like frisbies are usually the work of undisciplined young spooks. The O'Gools never allow their children to play such games.

Ghosti pops

Gloat's Glass

Skimmed milk

hic!

Miaow!

Work for Weirdos.

Shh!

At midnight it is time for work. Some places have to be haunted and Mr O'Gool, for one, would never let people down. He and Hairy clock in on the stroke of twelve every night.

Dog's Delight

Every dog has his night and tonight is mine!

The Haunting Hound.

Shh!!
Silence is essential for a successful haunting.

Daddy

Mona Ralph

Hairy really has disappeared

Ralph and Mona follow their father for a bit of fiendish fun. They practise uncanny screams and demonic laughs – but still fail to frighten anyone.

'They haven't the knack,' says their father, Fingal the Fearsome Phantom. He does not have high hopes for his children.

Hooligans a haunting

Mona and Ralph spend all night trying to distress the neighbours, ringing doorbells, tapping at windows, turning over dustbins. But it has no effect. People have grown used to things that go bump in the night. Nothing surprises them. Even the dogs and cats aren't scared of the two young ghouls. They might just as well have gone to school and learnt a bit from their elders.

A Haunting Song
Listen in the dark, listen in the dark
Cats wailing, dogs barking
Dustbins flying, doors banging
Floorboards creaking, taps dripping
Ghosts lurking, ghosts slipping
Silently through the night.

Crying
Cockles
and
mussels

A Night of Toils

With her husband gone a hauntin', Ginny is left at home
to play the role of bored houseghost. Light fingered, she
tinkles a rag on the grand piano while the hoover and the
broom and the duster dance in appreciation. Housework
is a hoot. She is a spook with a sparkle, a spectre with
splendour.

Meanwhile, Dad is hard at it, nose to the tombstone. In a
moment of weakness, he's left his job of haunting the
school and is down in the graveyard with a crowd of
disreputable, disembodied unearthly beings – his best
friends.

When Dad rolls home, he kisses his wife (and misses), tells Ralph and Mona they are too bad at haunting to miss a single night at school, tells Float and Gloat they are too young to disappear under his nose and upbraids Hairy and Scary for making themselves so scarce. Then he eats his supper and stands up, the better to tell them a ghost story. The Pie-Eyed Piper of Hamelin is their favourite. 'Once there was this piper . . .

.... hypnotised by
the piper,

the rats danced themselves to
death but this did not stop
them bopping. Their
ghosts dance on
for ever and
ever and
ever . . . . .

And at the end of the night the O'Gools say their prayers for the living and disappear. They float into a small iron box, bolt its door and wait for night to come again. If you find a locked box in your house do not try to open it.

You never know what will come out.

Good night, sleep tight.

The End